Watch out,
it's a mad dog!

"Come back here!" shouted Oliver. He pushed his bicycle through an opening in the fence and pedaled furiously to catch up. Oliver could see Bruiser heading for the ice-cream truck a block away. It was parked next to the children's playground. Bruiser sped up.

"Watch out, it's a mad dog!" a woman in dark glasses screamed. The children around the truck began to scatter. Inside the truck, the owner stared in horror.

Bruiser dived through the open door at the back of the truck. The truck rocked. Oliver raced over.

"Oh, no!" he cried. Bruiser's front paws were sitting in a tub of fudge ripple ice cream.

OLIVER'S LUCKY DAY

OLIVER'S LUCKY DAY

PAGE McBRIER

Illustrated by Blanche Sims

Troll Associates

Library of Congress Cataloging in Publication Data

McBrier, Page.
   Oliver's lucky day.

   Summary: When Oliver and his mother acquire a
Pekingese, hardly Oliver's idea of a "buddy," Oliver
starts a pet-care service so he can have a pet people
will respect.
   1. Children's stories, American. [1. Dogs—Fiction.
2. Pets—Fiction] I. Sims, Blanche, ill. II. Title.
PZ7.M47830n   1986   [Fic]   85-8437
ISBN 0-8167-0537-2 (lib. bdg.)
ISBN 0-8167-0538-0 (pbk.)

OLIVER'S LUCKY DAY

CHAPTER
1

Oliver Moffitt pressed his nose against the car window and hummed cheerfully. Today was his lucky day.

Oliver's mother looked over at him from the driver's seat and smiled. "Excited?" she asked. "I can't wait," he said. After years of asking, Oliver had finally convinced his mother that they needed a dog. He and the dog were going to be great buddies.

"Do you think the dog can sleep with me tonight?" asked Oliver. "It might be lonely and miss its brothers and sisters."

Oliver's mother turned the car into Copper Street and smiled. "I don't know. We'll have to let the dog decide that."

Oliver watched the stores along Copper Street move past slowly. "Which breed do you like best?" he asked. "Irish setters or golden retrievers?" Oliver was an expert on dogs and other pets. He had read dozens of pet books and had a room full of animal posters.

"I'm not sure I know the difference," replied Mrs. Moffitt.

"I'll show you when we get to the pet store," said Oliver. "What do you think of the name Thunder?"

"Why don't we just wait and see?" said Mrs. Moffitt. "The dog may already have a name."

Mrs. Moffitt pulled into the parking place near Perkins' Pet Supply. Oliver jumped out of the car as soon as it stopped.

"See you inside, Mom," he yelled. He raced to the store and stopped outside. He took a deep breath. In the display window was an unfriendly red parrot, which had been there ever since Oliver could remember. Today the parrot was surrounded by a pyramid of Chow Dog Food cans. Propped against them was a sign that said A PERKINS' SPECIAL! BUY 2 CANS GET 1 FREE! Oliver reminded himself to pick up a few cans on the way out.

He turned around to look for his mother. She waved to him from down the block. Oliver waved back. "I'll be back at the puppy cages," he shouted.

Oliver ran into the store and turned left at the tropical fish tanks. He usually stopped there to watch the piranhas, but not today.

At the rear of the store Oliver came to a long railing. It was supposed to keep people from going back to the dog cages and cat cages. Oli-

ver squeezed under the bar and began looking at some dachshund puppies.

"Young man," he heard a voice say, "what do you think that railing is for?"

"Good morning," Oliver said, turning to face a salesman. "I'm here to help my mother select a dog. Don't you have anything bigger than—"

"You'll have to move back," said the salesman.

"Sorry," said Oliver.

Mrs. Moffitt came up to the two of them. "Oh, aren't they cute?" She was looking at some cat-sized dogs in a cage.

"Those aren't real dogs," Oliver said. "They're Shih Tzus. A toy breed from China."

He turned to the salesman again. "Don't you have anything larger? Collies, Irish setters, golden retrievers?"

But the salesman wasn't listening. He was smiling at Mrs. Moffitt, who was holding one of the little dogs in her arms. It had a blue bow in its hair.

"Oh, Oliver, isn't this the cutest, sweetest, most adorable little thing you've ever seen?"

The dog began to smother Mrs. Moffitt's face with kisses. Its feet beat the air like paddles.

Oliver reached over to pet the dog. It glanced at him and growled.

"Please be careful," said the salesman. Oliver stuck his hands in his pockets.

"How much more will this particular Shih Tzu grow?" asked Oliver. He tried to sound as polite as he could.

"He's nearly full-grown now." The salesman

12

turned to Mrs. Moffitt and gave her another big smile. "That dog makes a perfect pet," he said to her. "He's small enough to carry anywhere. And he comes from a long line of pedigreed champions. Best of all, he's already housebroken."

"Oh, you cute, cutesie-wootsie." Mrs. Moffitt fingered the bow.

Oliver felt like throwing up.

"What's your name, little sweetheart?" Mrs. Moffitt asked the dog.

"Pom-pom," said the salesman. "That's from Madame de Pompadour, which is his mother's name."

"Oooh, and you look just like a little Pom-pom, don't you?" bubbled Oliver's mother.

Oliver pulled his mother aside. "Mom," he said, "small dogs with pushed-in noses like that can develop serious breathing problems."

"We'll take him!" Mrs. Moffitt said to the salesman.

"We haven't seen all the puppies yet," said Oliver.

Mrs. Moffitt gave the dog another kiss. "We're going to take you to our house, Pom-pom," she said. "Would you like that?" Pom-pom wiggled some more.

Oliver sighed and went to pick up some dog food. He shook his head when his mother asked him to help her pick out a leash and collar.

On the way home Pom-pom sat on Mrs. Moffitt's lap and whined.

"Mom," said Oliver, "do you think we made a mistake?"

"The poor little thing," said Mrs. Moffitt. "He's just frightened, that's all." Oliver couldn't see what was so frightening about his mother's lap. Pom-pom started to make choking sounds.

"I think he's going to get carsick," said Mrs. Moffitt. "Take him off my lap and put him on the floor. I'm going to try to pull over."

Oliver grabbed the dog to move him to the floor. It was too late. Pom-pom threw up—on Oliver.

"Yuck," said Oliver. "This is disgusting."

Mrs. Moffitt pulled off the road.

She handed Oliver a box of tissues. "Hop outside the car and try to clean yourself off. The poor little dog."

"What a mess," Oliver said to himself.

At the house Pom-pom spent the afternoon on Mrs. Moffitt's bed, recovering from the car ride.

Until Pom-pom had arrived, Oliver and his mother had lived alone. Oliver's parents were divorced, and he hadn't seen his father since he was a baby. His father lived in another city. His mother worked as a bookkeeper for an insurance company. That meant it was going to be Oliver's job to take Pom-pom for his afternoon walk.

Before dinner Oliver went upstairs to get Pom-pom ready for his first walk.

"Let's go, Pom-pom," said Oliver. Pom-pom wagged his tail as Oliver clipped the new rhine-

14

stone leash to his matching collar. They ran downstairs and out the door.

Over in the next yard Oliver's neighbor, Samantha Lawrence, was doing chin-ups on a branch. She was the best athlete in Oliver's class.

"Hi, Oliver," she called. "Did you get your new dog yet?"

"He's right here," said Oliver. He waggled the rhinestone leash.

"Where?" said Sam. "I don't see anything." She dropped from the branch and came over to investigate.

Pom-pom was curled up in a little lump at Oliver's feet.

Sam stared at the dog. "Is that Thunder?" she asked. Pom-pom looked up and growled.

"His name is Pom-pom," replied Oliver. "I don't think he likes kids."

"He looks more like a cat than a dog," said Sam.

"He's a Shih Tzu," said Oliver. "That's half Pekingese and half Lhasa apso. Mom fell in love with him, and there was nothing I could do."

Sam shook her head. "Small, isn't he?"

"Yeah," said Oliver.

That night at dinner Oliver opened a can of Chow Dog Food and measured out the right amount. Next to the canned food Oliver put a bowl of Chow Puppy Food.

"Here, Pom-pom," he called. "Take your

choice." Pom-pom ran over. He sniffed at each bowl once and walked away. He sat down on his new blue satin pillow.

"You can at least try one bite," said Oliver.

"Maybe it's too heavy for his delicate stomach," said Mrs. Moffitt. "Why don't you let him try our dinner?"

"Table scraps aren't good for dogs," said Oliver.

"But tuna-noodle casserole is very nutritious," said Mrs. Moffitt.

Oliver sighed and put a dish of casserole on the floor. Pom-pom gobbled it down.

At bedtime Oliver brushed his teeth and put on a clean pair of pajamas. He went downstairs and picked up the blue pillow.

"Mom, have you seen Pom-pom?" he asked.

Mrs. Moffitt shook her head. "I've never seen you ready for bed this early," she said. He kissed her good night.

"It's been a busy day," he said.

Oliver went up to his mother's room and found Pom-pom curled up on her bed.

"Would you like to sleep in my room tonight?" Oliver asked. He waved the pillow. Pom-pom didn't move.

"Maybe I'll just carry you in there and see how you like it," he said. Oliver lifted Pom-pom up carefully. "Ow! Watch it!" said Oliver when the dog snapped at him. He dropped Pom-pom on the bed. "Here's your dumb pillow." Oliver threw it down.

"What's going on?" called Mrs. Moffitt.

"Nothing," said Oliver. "I was jus[t] Pom-pom good night. See you in the morn[ing]

"Sweet dreams," said Mrs. Moffitt.

Oliver looked down at Pom-pom. "Some buddy you've turned out to be," he said.

telling
ing
"

CHAPTER
2

A few days later Oliver was sitting on the front steps with his best friend, Matthew Farley. They were discussing the Pom-pom problem.

"Maybe if you fed Pom-pom more meat, he'd grow a little," Matthew said. Matthew was the shortest kid in the fifth grade. His mother had told him that the more you ate, the taller you grew.

"It won't work. He's supposed to be small," replied Oliver. The two boys thought some more.

"Let's teach him some tricks," said Matthew. "How about fetching?"

"I tried that already," said Oliver. "When you throw something for him to fetch, he thinks you're trying to hit him with it. He hides under the bed."

Matthew thought some more. "How about a disguise?"

"I haven't seen too many dogs in disguises," said Oliver. Then he remembered the time long ago when his mother had taken him to the circus. One of the clowns had a little dog dressed in a clown costume. During the performance the clown-dog did amazing tricks like jumping through burning hoops and riding bareback on a horse.

"Maybe a disguise will give Pom-pom more confidence," Oliver said.

Oliver dashed up to his room. Over his desk hung a poster of popular dog breeds. On a bookshelf he had a collection of animal statues and a boxed book set entitled *Caring for Your Pet*. He had earned the money for this from his old newspaper route.

Oliver's most prized possession was a stuffed barn owl, which he had won last year in a science contest. For several weeks after he brought the owl home, Oliver was able to charge the other kids admission to his room.

Oliver rummaged through his closet until he found what he was looking for. He dashed downstairs. Matthew was pitching Doggy Treats to Pom-pom from across the living room.

"A werewolf mask?" said Matthew, looking up.

"It'll make him look ferocious," replied Oliver.

Pom-pom growled and hopped up on the sofa.

"Wow," said Oliver. "He likes it."

Matthew shook his head. "He looks pretty mad to me."

"No problem," said Oliver. He gave Pom-pom the mask to sniff.

Pom-pom was still growling. He gripped the rubber mask in his teeth and shook it. Oliver pulled the mask over Pom-pom's head. Pom-pom tried to pull it off with his paws.

"Come on, Matthew," said Oliver. "Let's take him for a walk and test the disguise."

"We can walk to the Quick Shoppe," said Matthew. He jangled some coins in his pocket. When he heard the word "walk," Pom-pom stopped struggling and ran to the door.

"Good idea," said Oliver. "Pom-pom has never been there before. I'll get his leash."

As they approached the Quick Shoppe the two boys could see several bicycles in the parking lot. Oliver knew the one with the reflectors on the spokes belonged to Rusty Jackson. Rusty was supposed to be in the seventh grade, but he had been held back. He liked to brag that he had already grown six inches this year. Rusty's two pals, Jay Goodman and Paul Patterson, also had their bicycles parked outside.

"Maybe we should come back another time," said Matthew.

"I'm not afraid of those guys," replied Oliver. He sailed through the front door. Rusty and his friends were over in the corner reading comic books.

Rusty looked up, stared at Pom-pom, and hooted. "What's *that* supposed to be?"

By now Pom-pom was pulling hard on the leash and growling. In his struggle Pom-pom

had turned the mask around so that the werewolf's eyes were in the back.

"Oliver," whispered Matthew, tugging at his sleeve, "I have to leave."

"What do you mean?" Oliver asked. "You can't go *now*."

"It's time for my trumpet lesson," Matthew said.

"Can't you be late?"

"I was late last time, and the teacher told my parents. I'm already in trouble for skipping out on my karate lesson. Sorry, Oliver." Matthew spun around and was gone.

Oliver looked over at Rusty again. Rusty stopped whispering to Jay and Paul.

"That's some pet you've got there," he said to Oliver. "What do you call it?"

"This is a cross between a wolf and a cat," answered Oliver. "They're ferocious. Haven't you ever seen one?"

"Not really," said Rusty. "Mind if I take a closer look?"

"I'd be careful if I were you," said Oliver, backing toward the door. He looked around wildly for Mr. Sanchez, the owner of the store. But the man was nowhere to be seen.

"Grab it, boys!" Rusty called. He shoved Oliver against the door. Jay grabbed Pom-pom, and Paul snatched off the mask.

The three boys burst out laughing. "So this is your ferocious pet," said Rusty. "It's nothing but a sissy-looking dog."

Oliver wrestled free from Rusty's hold. "You give him back."

"Make us," said Rusty. He dashed out the door. Oliver followed. "Come on, guys," Rusty shouted. Jay and Paul ran outside.

"Watch this, Oliver," said Jay. He held Pom-pom high in the air and tossed the dog to Paul. Pom-pom yapped in fear.

Oliver watched helplessly. The boys threw Pom-pom back and forth to one another like a basketball.

"Stop it. You'll hurt him," yelled Oliver.

Rusty stuffed Pom-pom under his arm and climbed onto his bicycle. "Okay, we'll stop. Good seeing you, Oliver." He turned to ride away.

"Wait," cried Oliver. "What about my dog?"

"What about him?" Rusty laughed. "My baby sister would love a sissy dog like this."

"But you can't take him. My mother will kill me."

"Well," Rusty said slowly, "maybe we can work something out." He put his other arm on Oliver's shoulder. "I've been thinking, Oliver," he said. "Sixth-graders have an awful lot of books to carry. It sure would be nice if I had someone *special* to help me with my heavy load."

Oliver gulped.

"I'll be glad to give your dog back if you help me out with my books. How about it?"

Oliver knew he'd been had.

*   *   *

That night at dinner Oliver barely touched his macaroni and cheese. He'd had to carry Pom-pom all the way home from the Quick Shoppe because the dog was too upset to walk.

"If I had a Doberman pinscher," Oliver muttered, "this would never have happened." He dreaded the next morning. He had promised Rusty he would meet him at his house and carry his books. Oliver's arms ached at the thought. He could only hope Rusty would get tired of the joke. But knowing Rusty, Oliver doubted it.

"Is something bothering you, Oliver?" asked Mrs. Moffitt. She set a saucer of macaroni and cheese on the floor for Pom-pom.

Oliver took a deep breath. "I need a dog," he said.

"But we have a dog."

"Pom-pom is not a real dog. He doesn't eat real dog food, he can't play fetch or roll over, and he's too short."

Pom-pom looked up from his macaroni and growled.

"Oliver," said Mrs. Moffitt, "I had no idea you felt this way. Why didn't you say something earlier?"

"I tried to, Mom, but you wouldn't listen."

Mrs. Moffitt sat and thought for a while. Finally she said, "I can understand why you're unhappy. But Pom-pom is part of our family now. We can't get rid of him."

"But why can't we just get another dog?" asked Oliver. "I promise I'll take care of it."

"I think you're going to have to learn to live with Pom-pom," said Mrs. Moffitt. "One pet is enough."

Oliver sighed and pushed his macaroni and cheese around with his fork. How was he ever going to have a pet of his own?

The next morning Oliver was ready to leave the house fifteen minutes early. "Where are you off to at this hour?" asked Mrs. Moffitt. "It's not like you to be so early."

"I promised someone I'd help him out this morning," said Oliver.

"That's very thoughtful of you," said Mrs. Moffitt. "Do I know this person?"

"I don't think so," said Oliver. "He's a lot older than me." He gave his mother a fast hug and ran out the door before she could ask any more questions.

When he got to Rusty's house, Oliver rang the bell. Mrs. Jackson answered the door.

"Good morning," said Oliver. "Is Rusty around?"

"Russell," called Mrs. Jackson, "one of your little friends is here." Oliver wished the entire fifth grade could have heard Rusty being called Russell. And Oliver being called his little friend.

Rusty came into the hall, carrying a load of school books. "Let's go," he snarled.

"Russell!" said Mrs. Jackson. "Is that any way to speak to a friend? You haven't even introduced us."

"This is Oliver," he said. Before Oliver could

say a word, Rusty shoved him out the door. He thrust the stack of books into Oliver's arms.

"Ow!" said Oliver, "What are you trying to do? Break my arms?"

Rusty climbed onto his bicycle. "Just shut up and do what I tell you," he said. "And don't try to get out of it, or you'll be sorry." Rusty laughed and rode off.

As Oliver struggled along, he thought about last night's conversation with his mother. This would never have happened if he had a pet people respected. Oliver wondered how he could get another pet.

Maybe I can work on Saturdays at the pet store, he thought. He didn't imagine that a real store would hire a ten-year-old, though, even if he *was* a pet-care expert. How about if I borrow a pet? Oliver thought. No. Who would want to lend out a pet?

Oliver stopped walking. "That's it!" he said. "I've got it. A way to have lots of pets without having any pets at all!"

CHAPTER
3

A little drop of sweat trickled down Oliver's nose as he stood on the front lawn, hammering away.

"Oliver," Mrs. Moffitt called from inside the house, "are you ever going to finish cutting the grass?"

"In a minute, Mom. I'm almost done with this."

Oliver looked down and smiled. Lined up like billboards on the lawn were three neatly lettered signs.

Oliver couldn't believe how smoothly everything had gone so far. When he'd told his mother he wanted to start a pet-care business, she'd liked the idea. And it was her suggestion to advertise his service in the school paper. Now that the word was out, the only thing Oliver needed was customers. He hoped they wouldn't all come at once.

Jennifer Hayes and Kimberly Williams walked by. They were in Oliver's class at school, and both had pets. Jennifer was wearing a Purple Worms T-shirt and chewing a wad of gum. Oliver wasn't sure, but it looked as if her eyelids were covered with sparkling purple eye shadow. Jennifer had a thing about purple. The Purple Worms were her favorite rock group, her bedroom was painted purple, and she usually chewed purple gum.

Kim looked more her age. She had three brothers and sisters. Her mother was the school librarian.

Oliver waved and called them over. "Hi, Jennifer and Kim! Have you heard about my new business?" he asked. Oliver wished that his business cards were ready.

"What business?" asked Jennifer. She blew a huge purple bubble and neatly popped it. Now that he could see her up close, Oliver was sure about the eye shadow.

"I've started a pet-care service," he said.

"Really?" said Jennifer. "Could you take care of my cat, Princess Fluffy?"

"Or my rabbit, Hopkins?" Kim asked.

Oliver pointed to his sign. "I'm good with dogs and good with cats. I'll even baby-sit your rats."

"Ugh! I would *never* own a rat," said Jennifer.

"Me neither," said Kim.

"Why should I let *you* take care of Princess Fluffy?" said Jennifer.

Oliver turned to Kim. One of her brothers had a boa constrictor.

"As I was saying," Oliver continued, "my service offers remarkable pet care at low cost." Oliver peered at Kim's eyelids. "Don't tell me *you're* wearing that stuff, too," he said.

Kim ignored him. "Do you come to my house, or do I bring my pet here?" she asked.

"I'll be happy to come to your house," he said. "Why don't you both come up to my office so I can give you some more information?"

"You have an office?" said Kim. "I'm impressed."

Oliver smiled. "Right this way," he said.

When they entered the house, Pom-pom came bouncing up to them. As usual he was barking.

"Ooooh, hello, Pom-pom," gurgled Jennifer. She and Kim knelt down to play with the dog. "You're so lucky, Oliver," Jennifer said.

"I guess," Oliver said.

"Look at the cute little ribbon in his hair," said Kim.

"I'll be in my office." Oliver sighed and went upstairs.

In his room Oliver surveyed the results of his labors. He had moved his desk around so that it faced the door. The stuffed owl had a sign hanging around its neck that said Oliver Moffitt—Pet-Care Expert. Mrs. Moffitt had agreed to let Oliver have his own phone installed if he used his profits to pay the bill. Next to the phone were neat stacks of paper and sharpened pencils. Oliver's popular-dog-breeds poster had been taped to the door. His pet-care books sat on his desk for ready reference.

Oliver kicked a pile of dirty laundry under the bed and gave his office a final inspection. The girls were still downstairs. "Are you coming or not?" he called.

"Hold on," said Jennifer. A minute later Kim came through the door. Jennifer followed, carrying Pom-pom. She was combing Pom-pom's hair with a pink comb. "We were playing with Pom-pom's hairdo," said Jennifer.

"Your owl looks great like that," said Kim.

"Thanks." Oliver reached into his desk drawer. "Perhaps you'd like some free literature," he said. Oliver handed Kim a piece of paper.

OLIVER'S PET-CARE SERVICE
RELIABLE PET CARE
BY AN EXPERT
DOG-WALKING
CAT-SITTING
BIRD-FEEDING
ETC.
REASONABLE PRICES
BIG DOGS ARE MY SPECIALTY
CALL 555-8058

"That's terrific," said Kim. "Do you have any customers?"

"Not yet," Oliver replied. "Maybe you can give one of my flyers to your brother."

Jennifer peered over Kim's shoulder. "I don't know if I'd trust you with my pet," she said. "Cats are very temperamental, you know. When I go away Princess Fluffy stays at Hermann's Pet Palace."

"That rip-off." Oliver hooted.

Jennifer's expression darkened. "Every time Princess Fluffy stays there, they give us a report card on her behavior," she said, putting down the pink comb. "She always makes straight A's."

"That place is a joke," said Oliver. "They give every pet straight A's just so you'll go back."

Jennifer's face screwed up into a tight mask. "What makes you think your pet service is any better?" she asked. She plopped Pom-pom down on Oliver's desk.

"Jennifer," said Oliver, "I am a pet-care expert. Since when do pets get grades? It's stupid."

Jennifer blew a big bubble and popped it with her finger. "Princess Fluffy is not stupid. She's a very smart cat. Don't you agree, Kim?"

"I guess so," said Kim.

"Besides," said Jennifer, "Princess Fluffy's a girl, and everyone knows girls are smarter than boys, and cats are smarter than dogs."

"That's crazy," said Oliver. "How can you possibly believe that?"

"Because it's true, that's why."

"Prove it," said Oliver.

36

"We don't have to prove it," said Jennifer. "Come on, Kim. Let's get out of here." The two girls stamped down the stairs.

Oliver looked at Pom-pom. "Stupid girls," he said. "I guess I didn't want their business, anyway."

CHAPTER
4

Oliver sat with his feet up on the desk in his office. He had the phone right beside him—in easy reach. His signs had been up for days, but he still didn't have any customers. He was just about to go downstairs and watch TV when he heard the phone ring. Oliver grabbed it.

'Oliver Moffitt, pet-care expert,'' he answered.

"Hello, Oliver," a voice said.

"Who is this?" Oliver asked.

"It's Josh. Who do you think?" Josh Burns was the smartest person in the class. He knew everything there was to know about computers. But Oliver knew he didn't own a pet.

"I called to find out how your business is doing," said Josh.

"Not so well," Oliver replied. "I still don't have any customers."

"Maybe you should advertise some more,"

said Josh. "There's a kid where my cousin lives who sells Yippee Yogurt Health Bars. He had all these little flyers made up and then slid them under people's doors."

"That's a great idea," Oliver said. "Maybe we could pass out my flyers in the neighborhood. Would you help me?"

"I suppose," replied Josh, "but I really want to stay home and finish my new computer program so I can try it out this weekend on my dad's office computer."

"It would be great exercise," said Oliver.

"You sound like my mother," Josh said.

"How about if I meet you in front of your house? I'll ride my bike over," Oliver said.

"All right," said Josh. "I guess I could help you."

Ten minutes later Oliver was cruising down Sutherland Avenue. He had stuffed his flyers into his bicycle basket and weighted them down with a rock. He turned the corner into Josh's street. Matthew was hurrying up the block toward him.

"Hey, Matthew, come help me and Josh pass out my pet-care flyers," Oliver yelled.

"I can't," said Matthew. "I'm on my way to my gymnastics class." Oliver pedaled past him, shaking his head.

When Oliver reached Josh's house, he went up to his room.

"Let's go, Josh," Oliver said. Josh got up from his desk and put away his notebook.

After about an hour the boys had given away

most of the flyers. Exhausted, they sprawled out next to a hedge on a lawn.

"That should do it," Josh said.

"No problem," Oliver replied. "I hope Mom is home from work by now to take phone calls." Oliver lay back in the grass. He was just about to close his eyes when a reflecting wheel flashed by. Rusty. For more than a week Oliver had been carrying Rusty's books to school every morning. He was sick of it.

As Rusty rode by he waved at Oliver. Oliver gave him a halfhearted smile.

"He's a bully," said Josh. "I don't like him."

"Me neither," said Oliver. He didn't want anyone to know he was carrying Rusty's books. "Come on," he said. "Let's finish those flyers."

"I still don't have any customers," Oliver told Josh on Friday.

"What you need is a gimmick," said Josh. "Something to capture people's imaginations. A giveaway item."

"I can't think of anything to give away, except Pom-pom," Oliver said.

Josh laughed. "How about a free treat for each pet you watch?" said Josh. "For instance, a bone for every dog and a fish head for every cat."

"Where am I going to keep all those bones and fish heads?" asked Oliver.

Josh didn't answer. Oliver thought a moment. "No problem!" said Oliver. "Mom will let me use the freezer, I bet."

"I can print out new flyers on my dad's computer this weekend," Josh said. "We can pass them out during lunch in the cafeteria on Monday."

"Great," said Oliver. "And let's wear the same clothes so people will notice us."

"How about red T-shirts, and baseball caps covered with weird buttons?" said Josh. "I've got a million that say things like KISS ME, STUPID, I ♥ COMPUTERS, HAVE YOU HUGGED YOUR PET TODAY?"

"You're on," said Oliver.

By Monday Oliver had painted a poster with pictures of bones and fish heads along with the words OLIVER WILL PAMPER YOUR PET. Carrying it carefully, he rushed to meet Josh before the bell.

He and Josh soon walked into class with the poster and button-covered hats.

"Where did you get those neat hats?" asked Matthew.

"It's an advertising ploy," said Josh.

Ms. Callahan, their teacher, had the boys come to the front of the room to explain their idea.

When lunch hour finally arrived, Oliver and Josh dashed to the cafeteria and set up their display. Oliver propped his poster against the wall and stood near the door. Josh was going to walk around the cafeteria with the flyers.

The first kids to arrive were the first-graders and second-graders. They giggled and pointed at the poster. Oliver ignored them.

When Oliver's class came through the lunch line, the kids all stopped to look.

"Nice work, Oliver," said Matthew.

Even Jennifer was polite. "Your poster looks nice," she said.

"You're a good artist," said Kim.

"Usually boys can't draw," Jennifer added.

When Sam came through, she started to do a cartwheel, but a teacher grabbed her arm and stopped her.

"Sorry about that," she said to Oliver. "I just wanted to attract some attention over here." She shrugged and got in line.

Out of the corner of his eye Oliver could see Josh walking around the cafeteria. Every few minutes he would stop and point at Oliver.

Oliver was so busy watching Josh that he didn't even notice the sixth-graders had started coming in.

"Well, if it isn't my friend Oliver."

Oliver froze. It was Rusty. Standing behind him were Jay and Paul. In the excitement Oliver had forgotten all about Rusty's books that morning.

"Where were you this morning?" asked Rusty. "Did you think if you didn't show up I'd just forget about you?"

Oliver was silent.

"What's this?" Rusty asked as he snatched a flyer. "Pet-care expert?" He showed the flyer to Jay and Paul. The three boys burst out laughing.

Oliver wished he could sink into the floor and disappear.

"I'll tell you what," Rusty said. "You've been very good about showing up to carry my books. I'll be willing to forget the whole thing if you just do me one more little favor."

"What's that?" Oliver asked nervously.

Rusty leaned over and flashed Oliver a mean smile. "Help me with my lunch tray, turkey."

Oliver started to protest, but Rusty gave him a shove and said, "Now!"

Oliver's mind raced as Rusty pushed him through the lunch line. How could he have forgotten about the books?

Rusty filled his tray with plates of franks and beans, creamed corn, and cherry cobbler. He took two cartons of milk. Then he turned and handed his full tray to Oliver.

"I'll be at that long table in the corner," he said. "Thanks, pal."

Rusty sat waiting as Oliver slowly picked his way through a maze of students. As he passed a crowded table near Rusty's, he looked down and saw a leg moving out.

Oliver tried to stop, but it was too late. He tripped. The tray flew through the air and landed on Rusty. Creamed corn dripped from Rusty's hair, and baked beans and cherry cobbler ran down his T-shirt. Everyone in the cafeteria laughed. Except Rusty.

He jumped out of his seat. "Boy, are you going to regret this," he said as he stomped out of the cafeteria.

Oliver gulped and looked down. The leg that

had tripped him was still there. He looked up into the face of Wally Perona, a sixth-grader.

"Nice work, kid," said Wally. "I'm looking for someone to walk my dog Wednesday after school. You interested?" Wally was the biggest boy in school. No one except Oliver had seen that Wally had tripped him.

"Good job, Oliver," Sam yelled from the other side of the cafeteria.

"So," Wally said, "are we on for Wednesday afternoon?"

"You bet!" Oliver said with a smile. "I'll be happy to walk your dog."

On the way back to class Josh and Matthew rushed over to Oliver.

"What happened? What did Wally say?" asked Josh.

"Did you spill that tray on purpose?" said Matthew. "You really got Rusty good."

Oliver grinned. "I have a customer," he said.

"You mean Wally?" said Josh. "Wow!"

"I'm impressed, Oliver," said Matthew.

It wasn't long before the news about Rusty was all over school.

CHAPTER
5

Oliver rushed down to the kitchen for breakfast. This was the day he was going to walk Wally's dog.

"Mmmm, pancakes!" he said and hugged his mother.

Mrs. Moffitt smiled. "I thought they'd bring you luck," she said. She put two plates on the table and sat down.

"Thanks, Mom," said Oliver, digging in. "These are great. Did you have a chance to pick up a bone at the butcher's?"

"Oh, I'm glad you reminded me." Mrs. Moffitt went to the refrigerator and took out some neatly wrapped packages from the freezer. "Here you are," she said. "Just as you ordered. Each package has a beef leg bone, cut into a three-inch piece and boiled for fifteen minutes."

"Nice work, Mom. Thank you," said Oliver. "You sound like a pet-care expert yourself."

Mrs. Moffitt laughed and sat down again. "I have a good teacher," she said. "I'm still not sure about those fish heads, though."

"No problem," said Oliver. "As long as they're frozen, they won't stink."

Oliver helped himself to more pancakes. "I'll need extra energy today," he said, pouring on the syrup. He gave Pom-pom a bit of pancake under the table.

"Don't forget to keep an eye on Pom-pom," said Mrs. Moffitt.

"No problem," he replied. "I'll walk him after I finish walking Wally's dog."

Mrs. Moffitt stopped eating. "I thought you were taking Pom-pom with you."

"I can't show up at Wally's with Pom-pom. I'm on the job."

Mrs. Moffitt frowned. "That poor little dog is counting on you to take him out right after school. If you don't have time to walk him, you'll have to take him out with you."

"But, Mom—" Oliver began.

"Don't argue," said his mother. "Pom-pom is still your first responsibility."

Oliver walked over to the trash bin. He threw out the last of his pancakes. Maybe this wasn't going to be such a good day after all.

At school Oliver couldn't keep his mind on his work. During social studies he opened his desk top and pulled out the piece of paper with Wally's address. As he stared at the paper,

Oliver's mind began to wander. How many dog breeds can I count? he wondered. He was already up to nineteen when he heard Ms. Callahan call his name.

"Pekingese," said Oliver. The class started to giggle. Oliver could feel his face turning red.

"Pekingese is the capital of Iowa?" said Ms. Callahan. "Please pay attention, Oliver," she said with a smile.

Jennifer raised her hand.

"Yes, Jennifer?" said Ms. Callahan.

"Des Moines is the capital of Iowa, Ms. Callahan," she said. Jennifer looked over at Oliver and smirked.

"Teacher's pet," he said under his breath.

At last school was out. Oliver hopped on his bicycle.

"Good luck," Sam yelled.

"Thanks!" said Oliver, riding past her.

He was almost out of the parking lot when Rusty raced his bicycle around the corner and screeched to a stop.

"Where do you think you're going?" Rusty asked.

"Get out of my way, Rusty," said Oliver. "I'm in a hurry."

"Not anymore," said Rusty. He blocked Oliver's bicycle with his.

A car pulled up next to them. "Hello, boys," said Ms. Callahan.

"Hi, Ms. Callahan," said Oliver. He walked his bicycle around Rusty's and over to the car window. "I really liked that film we saw today on the life cycle of the butterfly."

"Did you?" said Ms. Callahan. "I'm so glad."

"It was very educational," Oliver said as he climbed back on his bicycle.

"See you tomorrow, Ms. Callahan," he said.

"Good-bye, Oliver," Ms. Callahan replied.

Before Rusty could do anything, Oliver sped off.

Pom-pom was waiting for Oliver. "Let's go," he said as he scooped up the dog. "We're going for a bike ride. Would you like that?" Pom-pom tried to wriggle out of Oliver's arms. "Oh, no, you don't!" he cried.

Oliver ran to the kitchen and gave Pom-pom a couple of Doggy Treats. Then he took one of the bones out of the freezer. "We can't be late for Wally's," he said. Oliver rushed back outside and stuffed Pom-pom and the bone into his bicycle basket. Pom-pom snarled.

"Aw, cut it out," said Oliver. "It'll be fun to ride in there."

Oliver climbed onto his bicycle and headed down the street. "That's not so bad, is it?" he said to Pom-pom. Pom-pom peeked out and whimpered.

About ten minutes later Oliver turned onto Maple Avenue. "Four-fifty," said Oliver. "This should be the place." He parked the bicycle on the sidewalk and made sure his shirt was tucked in.

"You be good and stay here," he told Pom-pom. "I'll be back soon with a *real* dog."

Oliver walked up and rang the bell. Wally answered the door.

"Come in, Moffitt," he said, his mouth full of food. He led Oliver to the kitchen. "Sit down."

Wally sat himself on a high stool at the kitchen counter. Oliver climbed up on one next to him. Wally pointed to a bag of potato chips. "Want some?" Oliver shook his head. Wally took a couple of chips and dunked them in an onion dip.

"So you're a pet-care expert," Wally said. He crammed the chips into his mouth.

"The best," said Oliver.

Wally nodded, still chewing. Finally he said, "I have to visit my grandmother this afternoon. All you have to do is take Bruiser for a nice, long walk." Wally slid off the kitchen stool. He went over to the basement door.

"Here, Bruiser!" Wally yelled down the stairs.

A dog that seemed as big as a horse came charging into the kitchen. Oliver gripped the edge of his stool.

"Is that a Saint Bernard?" he asked.

"He's a mix," replied Wally. "Part sheep dog, part Saint Bernard, and some Great Dane."

Bruiser bounded over to Oliver, stood on his hind legs, and plopped his front paws on the counter. He gave Oliver a sniff, then licked the bowl of onion dip clean.

"Sit, boy," said Wally. Bruiser flopped down. His tail wiped the floor like a dishrag. A kitchen stool went flying.

Wally walked over to the refrigerator. Bruiser's head jerked up.

"Okay, boy, it's snack time," Wally said. Bruiser gave a booming bark and rushed over.

"Down, boy," said Wally. He opened the door and took out bread, tomatoes, and a bag of marshmallows. *Thump, thump.* Bruiser's tail banged against the refrigerator door. Wally walked over to the counter and spread everything out. He tossed a marshmallow to Bruiser. It disappeared in his enormous jaws.

Wally made a stack of sandwiches. He turned and fed one to Bruiser. Bruiser swallowed it in one gulp. Wally ate the next sandwich. It disappeared nearly as fast as the one Bruiser ate.

"You sure you're not hungry, Moffitt?" Wally asked.

"No, thanks," replied Oliver. "I've never seen a dog eat tomato-and-marshmallow sandwiches before," he said.

"He loves 'em," said Wally.

Bruiser and Wally polished off the plate of sandwiches in less than three minutes. Wally looked at the kitchen clock.

"Time for me to go," he said. "Here's the key to the back door. You can leave it under the mat. Bruiser's leash is on the basement door. Anything else you need to know?"

"No problem," said Oliver. "I'm a dog owner myself."

Wally scratched Bruiser behind the ears. "So long, pup," he said. Bruiser whined a little as

Wally headed out the door. Oliver was on his own.

Oliver stood at one end of the kitchen and faced Bruiser. "Here, boy," he said.

Bruiser charged across the kitchen, jumped up, and planted his paws on Oliver's shoulders. Oliver crashed to the floor. The dog started to lick his face.

"Down, boy!" said Oliver, struggling to his feet. Bruiser wagged his tail.

"Let's go for a walk," Oliver said.

Bruiser boomed with joy and knocked Oliver over again. Oliver ran to the basement door.

After Oliver attached Bruiser's leash to his collar, Bruiser dragged him out the front door, across the front lawn, and over to the nearest tree. Pom-pom peeked out of the bicycle basket.

"Look, Pom-pom, this is a real dog," Oliver said. Pom-pom growled. Oliver pulled Bruiser toward the bicycle. "This way, Bruiser." Bruiser dragged Oliver in the opposite direction. "Come on, boy, let's go," said Oliver. Bruiser sniffed at the tree. Oliver tied Bruiser's leash to a branch.

He leaned down and scratched Bruiser behind the ears. "How am I going to keep up with you?" he asked. "I'll need a skateboard." Bruiser strained at his leash as a cat walked by. "Would you like me to walk you while I ride my bike?" asked Oliver. "That way you can pull as hard as you want."

Bruiser licked Oliver's face. Oliver wiped his face on his sleeve and got on his bicycle.

He untied Bruiser's leash from the tree and

slipped it over the handlebars. "Giddap!" he said. Bruiser trotted off.

As they rolled down the middle of the sidewalk, Oliver hung on easily. "I don't even need to pedal," he said to Pom-pom. Bruiser set a steady pace and ran easily. Pom-pom poked his head out to look around. Oliver started to hum.

When they got to the corner Bruiser turned left onto Dewey Place. "You lead the way, Bruiser," said Oliver. For the next few minutes Bruiser kept to a comfortable trot. All at once Bruiser perked up his ears. Oliver could hear a faint tinkling sound in the distance.

"What is it, Bruiser?" asked Oliver. "Do you hear that ice-cream truck?"

At the words "ice cream" Bruiser gave a yelp and flattened his ears. He took off at a gallop.

Oliver hung on for dear life as Bruiser pulled him toward the sound of the bells.

"Whoa, boy, whoa, boy!" he yelled. Bruiser kept going. He plowed across an empty ball field and skidded through a mud puddle. Oliver's teeth rattled as the bicycle shuddered through potholes. Houses and street signs grew blurred. Pom-pom burrowed deep in the basket.

"Sit, Bruiser," Oliver yelled. Bruiser galloped faster.

"I can't hold on much longer," Oliver yelled. They wheeled through an empty lot. Oliver ducked under a branch. Bruiser veered and headed straight for a fence. "Help!" screamed Oliver.

Oliver yanked the leash off the handlebars

and hit the brakes. He screeched to a halt. Bruiser jumped the fence and ran on.

"Come back here!" shouted Oliver. He pushed the bicycle through an opening in the fence and pedaled furiously to catch up. Oliver could see Bruiser heading for the ice-cream truck a block away. It was parked next to the children's playground. Bruiser sped up.

"Watch out, it's a mad dog!" a woman in dark glasses screamed. The children around the truck began to scatter. Inside the truck the owner stared in horror.

Bruiser dived through the open door at the back of the truck. The truck rocked. Oliver raced over.

"Oh, no!" he cried. Bruiser's front paws were sitting in a tub of fudge ripple ice cream. An overturned carton of vanilla ice cream was lying on the floor.

"Bruiser, how could you?" cried Oliver. Bruiser wagged his tail and barked.

"Get your dog out of here!" the owner yelled. He was wedged in a corner.

"He's not my dog," said Oliver. "He's—"

"I don't care who he belongs to. Just get him out!"

Oliver took hold of Bruiser's leash and pulled. Bruiser set his paws and didn't budge.

"Please, please, puh-leeze," begged Oliver. "We have to get out of here."

The children came back to watch. "Look, Mommy," said a boy, "big doggy eat ice cream."

"Isn't that the Perona dog?" asked a man wearing a baseball cap.

"Watch out," Oliver heard the woman in the dark glasses say. "Here comes another one." Pom-pom jumped out of the basket and into the truck.

"Pom-pom, get out of there!" Oliver screamed.

Pom-pom snapped at Bruiser's heels. Bruiser's nose was buried in fudge ripple ice cream. He spread his legs to get away from Pom-pom's teeth.

"*Yap, yap, yap*," Pom-pom barked. He nipped at Bruiser's paws until they moved again. Bruiser lifted his front paws out of the fudge ripple and began to back up. Oliver stared as Pom-pom nipped at Bruiser until he jumped down from the truck. Oliver grabbed Bruiser's leash.

"Good dog, nice puppy," said Oliver to Bruiser.

The owner of the truck hopped down. "Your dog just ruined a lot of ice cream, son. What do you plan to do about it?"

"I'm really sorry, sir," said Oliver. "It was an accident. I'll pay for whatever he ate."

"You're lucky most of the ice cream was in closed containers," the man said. "It shouldn't be too bad. Here, write down your name and address for me." He handed Oliver a piece of paper.

Oliver handed him his business card. "I'm really sorry," he said again. He could see his profit melting away like warm ice cream.

"Just don't let it happen again," said the

owner. "You nearly scared away all my customers."

Oliver grabbed his bicycle and Bruiser's leash. Pom-pom was still running in little circles around Bruiser's feet, yapping and snapping.

Oliver looked at Bruiser. "Bruiser!" he said. "You're covered with ice cream. I can't take you home all sticky. Wally won't ever hire me again. I'll be ruined."

He picked up Pom-pom and put him into the basket.

"Come on, Pom-pom," he said. "Let's go home first. Bruiser needs a bath."

CHAPTER
6

Now that Bruiser had had dessert, Oliver thought he seemed easier to control. When they rode up to Oliver's house, the pet-care expert took a closer look at the big dog.

"Boy, you sure are a mess," he said. "It's a good thing we still have time to clean you up before Mom gets home. I don't know how she'd feel about having you in our bathtub."

Oliver hurried up the front steps. "Bruiser, you stay here," he said, tying the leash to the porch railing. "We'll be back in a minute." Bruiser whined a little and sat down.

Oliver and Pom-pom dashed up to the bathroom. Oliver threw down the rubber bath mat and plugged the tub. Then he started to fill the tub with lukewarm water.

"Let's see," Oliver said. "The water should

come up to Bruiser's elbows, which is right about here." He turned off the faucet.

"Now for our bath supplies." Oliver walked over to the bathroom closet. "Cotton to keep the water out of Bruiser's ears, a washcloth for his face, and lots of clean towels." Oliver set everything on the floor. "What else?"

Pom-pom barked and ran in a little circle. "Right," said Oliver. "Dog shampoo." He rummaged through the closet until he found a pink-and-blue bottle. "Puppy Potion—Perfumed Shampoo for Your Pet," he read. "Yuck. This stuff stinks. I guess it'll have to do, though."

Oliver went to his room, kicked off his shoes, and changed into his bathing suit. "I don't need to do this when I bathe you, Pom-pom," said Oliver. "You don't splash enough."

Oliver was ready. He and Pom-pom went back outside and untied Bruiser's leash. Bruiser jumped up and knocked Oliver down.

"Calm down, boy," Oliver said, struggling to his feet. He carefully stuck two wads of cotton in Bruiser's ears. "That's to keep the water out," he said. "Now, are you ready for your bath?"

Bruiser flattened his ears and growled. Oliver gave the leash a tug. Bruiser sat down.

"What's the matter?" he asked. "Don't you like baths?"

Bruiser flattened his ears again and whined.

"Aw, come on," said Oliver. He gave Bruiser's leash another tug. Bruiser snarled and looked at the street.

Oliver put his hands on his hips. "You think

64

you can outsmart me, don't you?" he said. "Watch this. Here, Pom-pom," Oliver called. "I have someone who needs to be moved upstairs pronto to the B-A-T-H."

Pom-pom charged over. He flew around Bruiser's paws like a floor polisher. "*Yap, yap, yap,*" he barked.

Bruiser looked at Pom-pom and snarled. Then he lay down and folded his paws under his body. "Smart dog," said Oliver.

He studied Bruiser. "Now what? A pet-care expert never gives up!" Bruiser looked at a buzzing fly with interest.

"You think you're clever, don't you?" he said to Bruiser. "Well, this is going to be no problem." Oliver ran down to his bicycle and pulled out the bone from the basket. "Why didn't I think of this earlier?" Oliver went up the front steps and waved the bone under Bruiser's nose.

"Look what I have," he said. "Nice, juicy bone."

Bruiser sniffed the bone and put his head down between his paws.

Oliver looked at his watch. It was already four-thirty. His mother would be home in an hour.

"Bruiser," he said, "stop being so childish. You are going for a bath, and you are going now."

Oliver tugged on the leash. Bruiser started to yowl. Oliver put his hands over his ears and thought fast.

"Of course," Oliver said. "That's it!"

Oliver tied Bruiser's leash to the railing and ran to the freezer. He dug through frozen food and ice-cube trays, hoping he was right. In the back of the freezer Oliver felt a long box. He gave a tug and pulled. Success! It was a box of ice-cream pops.

Oliver grabbed a handful of pops and ran back outside. Bruiser perked up his ears.

"Now look what I have," Oliver said, waving the pops under Bruiser's nose. Bruiser stood up and bit at the ice cream.

Oliver snatched the pops away. "So you're still hungry for ice cream?"

He propped open the front door. "Stand back, Pom-pom," Oliver said. Bruiser tugged at his leash and whined. Oliver leaned forward to unsnap the leash. He gently waved the pops under Bruiser's nose.

"All these can be yours," he said, "if you just follow me."

Oliver began to count down. "Five, four, three, two, one!" He released the leash and raced up the stairs. Bruiser was hot on his heels. When he reached the bathtub, Oliver jumped in. Bruiser landed in the tub with a splash a second later.

Bruiser lunged at Oliver, who dropped the pops into the water. Bruiser polished them off, wrappers and all. *"Arf, arf,"* he barked, wagging his tail and nudging the floating sticks with his nose.

"No problem," said Oliver. He stepped briskly out of the tub. "Now all I have to do is shampoo you."

Bruiser hopped out of the tub.

"No, Bruiser," Oliver said. "You stay in the tub." Bruiser began to shake the water off. "Good grief," said Oliver. "There's more water outside the tub than inside." He made a grab for Bruiser, but Bruiser wedged himself behind the tub.

"Get back in the tub," said Oliver. "You're flooding the bathroom."

Pom-pom, who had been crouched in a corner, dashed over to the sink and started to bark. Bruiser looked worried.

Oliver ran into his office and picked up the phone. He dialed Matthew's number. While the phone was ringing, Oliver peeked around the corner at the bathroom. He could see a stream of water leaking out into the hall. Pom-pom was yapping his head off.

Matthew's mother answered the phone. "Is Matthew home?" asked Oliver. "This is Oliver calling." His teeth began to chatter from the cold.

"He's at his karate lesson," said Matthew's mother.

"Will he be home soon?" Oliver asked.

"In about an hour. Would you like me to give him a message?"

"No thanks," Oliver said. He hung up the phone and looked down at the puddle of water at his feet.

Oliver tried Josh's number next. Josh's mother said he was working on a special computer program at his father's office.

Time was running out. Oliver thought fast.

He needed to find someone who lived nearby and was strong. "Why didn't I think of her sooner?" he cried. He picked up the phone once more and dialed.

"Sam here." Oliver sighed with relief.

"It's me. Oliver," he said. "I'm having an emergency."

"Do you want me to call the police?" said Sam.

"No, I want you to come over," said Oliver. "I'm having trouble with one of my customers." Oliver could see Bruiser tiptoeing toward the hall stairs.

"I can't talk anymore," Oliver said. "Just come as soon as you can. *Please.*" He slammed down the phone and went to grab Bruiser.

When Sam arrived several minutes later, Oliver was still trying to push Bruiser into the bathroom.

"What's up?" asked Sam.

"It's Bruiser Perona," said Oliver. "He desperately needs a bath, but he just won't cooperate."

Sam rolled up her sleeves and looked Bruiser in the eye.

"You poor puppy," she said. "Come over here."

Bruiser sat down and let Sam scratch him between the ears.

"So you don't like baths," she said, kneeling down. Bruiser flattened his ears and whimpered.

"He only likes junk food," said Oliver. "Ice cream, marshmallows. Stuff like that." Bruiser whined.

Sam stared at Bruiser. "I don't think I've ever seen such a gooey-looking dog before," she said.

"It's I-C-E C-R-E-A-M," Oliver spelled. "He accidentally got some on his coat."

Sam stood up. "You're right. He definitely needs a bath," she said. "Wally wouldn't want him back this way."

Sam bent her knees, and with Oliver's help she picked up Bruiser. They carried him over to the tub, then lowered him into the water. Bruiser tried to bolt for the door. "Oliver, help me hold him," cried Sam, grabbing the dog.

"Sit, Bruiser," said Oliver. While Sam held Bruiser's front, Oliver pushed down the dog's rear. Bruiser sat with a splash.

"Get me the shampoo, Oliver," said Sam. Oliver poured it on Bruiser, and Sam worked up a lather.

"*We love you Camp Colorado, high in the Rocky Mountains,*" she sang. Sam went away to camp every summer for four weeks. The music seemed to calm Bruiser down.

After ten minutes of Sam's scrubbing and camp songs, Bruiser started to look clean. "Now for your final rinse," said Sam. She poured pails of clean water over Bruiser again and again. "Squeaky clean," she said at last and drained the tub. Bruiser stood up.

"Look out!" shouted Oliver. "He's going to shake! That's how he flooded the bathroom before."

"Sit, Bruiser," said Sam. Bruiser sat. "Oliver, hand me a big towel."

71

Sam took the towel Oliver handed her and wrapped it around Bruiser's middle. Then she closed the shower curtain. "Now you can shake," she said to him.

As Bruiser let loose behind the curtain, Sam sang, "Go, Bruiser, go. Let's fight, fight, fight. Bruiser's team will win tonight!" When Bruiser finished shaking, Sam opened the curtain, took another towel, and rubbed him dry. She cleaned out the inside of his ears with the cotton wads.

"Now you look beautiful," she said. Bruiser licked her face.

With Oliver's help Sam lifted Bruiser out of the tub and cleaned up the bathroom. Oliver piled the towels in the tub.

"I'll take care of them later," he said. "Why don't we dry him off a little more with my mom's hair dryer? We don't want him to catch cold."

"Great idea," said Sam.

Maybe it was the warm air from the dryer that calmed Bruiser down, maybe it was Sam's camp songs. In any case Bruiser left Oliver's house as peacefully as a lamb. On the way back to Wally's, Sam said, "It must be lots of hard work to be a pet-care expert."

Oliver thought about his afternoon and said, "It's really no problem." Bruiser bumped into Oliver, nearly knocking him down. "No problem at all."

CHAPTER
7

Matthew and Josh ran up to Oliver and Sam at lunch the next day. "How did it go?" he asked. "My mother said you called."

"Was everything all right?" asked Josh. "My mom said you called, too."

"Everything was fine," Oliver told them. "Wally's dog was a perfect gentleman. I took him for a nice long walk, fed him a snack, and then gave him a bath."

"Wow," said Matthew. "I wish I could have been there. I never get to do anything that's fun."

"Sam helped with the bath," Oliver said. "I couldn't have done it without her." Sam bowed.

"Have you given Wally your bill?" Josh asked.

"Not yet," he replied. "I'm going to bill on the first of each month. It's more professional."

"I helped him figure it out on the computer," Josh said.

"Right," said Oliver. "I've got some expenses, too."

Wally walked over to their table.

"Nice job, Moffitt," said Wally. He shook Oliver's hand. "By the way," he said, "did you give Bruiser a bath?"

"A little extra touch," said Oliver. "No charge."

Wally smiled. "Excellent," he said. "If you ever need anything from me, just let me know." Wally walked back to the sixth-graders.

When Oliver got home from school, he could hear Pom-pom throwing himself against the front door. "Calm down," Oliver said. Pom-pom dashed out and began nipping playfully at Oliver's shoes.

"Quit showing off," said Oliver. Pom-pom looked up and barked. "You want to go to the Quick Shoppe? I'm supposed to meet the gang there for a celebration." Pom-pom wagged his tail and yapped. "I guess I owe you a big thank you," Oliver said.

Kim and Jennifer were sitting on the curb when Oliver and Pom-pom arrived at the Quick Shoppe. They were listening to a Purple Worms tape on a recorder and drinking sodas.

"Everyone else is inside," said Kim.

"I'll watch Pom-pom for you," said Jennifer. She picked up Pom-pom and began kissing him.

Oliver went into the store.

"Hi, Oliver," said Sam. She, Josh, and Mat-

76

thew were loading up on sodas, chips, and peanut clusters.

"We'll meet you out on the curb," said Josh.

Oliver bought a soda and some pretzels and went outside. He could see reflecting wheels coming toward him.

"Oh, no, it's Rusty," said Sam. She and Kim groaned, and everyone started to laugh.

"What's so funny?" growled Rusty as he rode up. When no one answered, Rusty spun around and popped a few wheelies.

"Just ignore him," said Kim.

Rusty circled by again. This time he wasn't using his hands. "Why's everyone sitting here?" Rusty asked.

"If you must know, we're celebrating Oliver's new business," said Jennifer. Pom-pom, who had been sunning himself behind the Quick Shoppe, darted around the corner.

When Pom-pom saw Rusty, he whimpered and rolled over on his back.

Rusty laughed. "Some pet expert," he said. "Look at that dog. He's a complete wimp."

"He is not," said Oliver. "In ancient China Shih Tzus were called Tibetan lion dogs. They were used to guard palaces."

Rusty pretended to fall off his bicycle. "Help!" he cried. "I'm being attacked by a ferocious Chinese lion dog!" Rusty clutched his leg and fought off an imaginary dog.

"Very funny," said Sam.

Oliver made a face. "Shih Tzus happen to be super fast, Rusty," he said.

"Hah!" replied Rusty. "That little runt couldn't catch me if he tried."

Oliver's eyes narrowed. "You wanna bet?" he asked. Oliver felt Matthew poke him in the ribs.

"Are you kidding?" said Rusty. "I can run faster than a dog any day." He spun around and did another wheelie.

Oliver jumped up to face Rusty. "Let's bet then," he said. He saw Rusty look at him and hesitate.

"Why would I want to race a little dog?" asked Rusty.

"What's the matter?" Kim asked. "Are you afraid of him?"

Rusty spit on the street. "It's stupid," he said. "Anyone can beat him."

"I'll give you an advantage then," said Oliver. "I'll let you ride your bike."

Rusty stared at Oliver. "You want me to race that little runt on my bike? That's no contest."

Matthew grabbed Oliver's arm. "Are you crazy?" he whispered.

Oliver ignored Matthew. "Pick your prize, Rusty," he said.

Rusty thought for a moment and shrugged. "How about your stuffed owl?" he said. "I might as well make it worth my while."

Oliver swallowed hard. "All right," he replied. "But if Pom-pom wins I want your bike."

Rusty kicked the curb with his foot. "This is stupid," he said. "Your dog doesn't stand a chance."

"What are you afraid of, then?" asked Kim.

"I'm not afraid!" Rusty shouted. He turned to Oliver. "When do you want to run this race?"

Oliver smiled. "Friday after school in the parking lot over there," he said. "My dog needs time to train."

"I'll say," muttered Josh.

"Fine," said Rusty. He spun around the parking lot once more. "Stupid kids!" he yelled over his shoulder.

When Rusty was out of sight, everyone began to talk at once.

"Are you sure you know what you're doing?" asked Kim.

"Maybe you can get out of it," said Josh.

Oliver held his ground. "Shih Tzus are very fast," he said. "Watch this." Oliver marched to the other end of the parking lot.

"Here, Pom-pom," he called. Pom-pom looked at Oliver and barked. Then he rolled over and whimpered.

Jennifer shook her head. "I told you cats were smarter than dogs," she said. "Princess Fluffy always comes when I call."

"I'll try again," said Oliver. He clapped his hands and smiled. "Come here, Pom-pom." This time Pom-pom ran away from Oliver as fast as he could.

Oliver walked back to the curb. "Now what?" he asked.

"I'd say forget it," said Matthew.

"Maybe you can be sick on Friday," suggested Kim.

Josh looked at Oliver and shook his head. "Good luck, Oliver."

"You'll need it," added Jennifer.

Everyone got up and headed off. "Some celebration," said Oliver to Pom-pom when he trotted over to him.

"Thanks to Jennifer's big mouth," Oliver told Sam on the way to lunch the next day, "the news of the race is all over the school."

"You must feel terrible," Sam said.

Oliver nodded. "After my big success with Bruiser, Rusty is about to ruin everything. What am I going to do?" he asked.

"Don't worry," said Sam. "We'll think of something."

Oliver and Sam picked up their lunch trays and started to move through the line.

"Maybe we can fool him," said Oliver. He reached for a peanut-butter-and-jelly sandwich.

"How?" Sam grabbed a cup of turkey-noodle soup.

"If we could just think of a way to keep Pom-pom on a straight course," Oliver said. He stuck his hand into the cooler and pulled out an ice-cream pop. "There must be a way." Oliver stared at the ice cream, thinking. "Sam," he said, "I have a plan." He leaned over and whispered in her ear.

Sam's eyes widened. "Do you think it'll work?" she asked.

"Yes, I do," said Oliver. "But I'll need your

help. Can you meet me at my house after school?"

"Of course," said Sam. "What are friends for?"

Oliver picked up his tray. Humming cheerfully, he headed for the lunch table.

CHAPTER
8

"Well, Pom-pom," Oliver whispered, "today is race day." He fed Pom-pom an extra bowl of oatmeal and gave him a long scratch behind the ears.

"You certainly have been nice to Pom-pom recently," said Mrs. Moffitt. "Have you had a change of heart?"

"He's not so bad," said Oliver.

When Oliver walked into class, Josh came running over. "Today's the big day," he said. "Are you still going to race?"

"Absolutely," said Oliver. "Are you still going to be the judge?"

"Yes," said Josh. "I just hope you know what you're doing."

"Don't worry," said Oliver. "Just judge the race fairly."

Matthew walked in. "Hi, Oliver. Hi, Josh."

He let out a big sigh and threw his books on his desk. "I can't make it," he said.

"Make what?" asked Josh.

"The race," replied Matthew. "I've got choir practice."

"When did you start taking choir?" asked Oliver.

"It's my mother's idea," replied Matthew. "She thinks it'll help me get into a good college." Matthew sighed again. "I always miss out on the excitement."

Jennifer and Kim came over. "Hi, everybody," said Jennifer. "Going to the big race?"

"Of course," replied Josh. "Aren't you?"

"I'm going to be a cheerleader," she said.

Matthew, Josh, and Oliver looked at one another.

"Who are you cheering for?" asked Matthew.

Jennifer gave him one of her biggest smiles. "I'll cheer for the team most likely to win, of course. I already have my outfit picked out."

"That means Rusty," said Matthew. "You know Pom-pom doesn't stand a chance."

"Now wait a minute," said Oliver.

Jennifer put her hands on her hips. "It's a free country," she said. "I can cheer for anyone I want."

Oliver turned to Kim. "And I guess you'll do whatever Jennifer does, right?"

Kim looked at Jennifer. "No," she said.

"No?" Jennifer and Oliver said at the same time.

"No," said Kim. "Oliver and Pom-pom are

84

my friends, and I'll cheer for them no matter what."

"But Kim," said Jennifer, "I thought you were my best friend."

"I am," replied Kim. "But that doesn't mean I have to do everything you do."

"Forget it, then," said Jennifer. "I'll find another best friend." She walked off angrily.

Oliver turned to Kim again. "Gee, thanks, Kim," he said. "That was really nice of you to stick up for us."

"That's okay," she replied. "Sometimes Jennifer gets on my nerves."

"There's the bell," Matthew said. "We'd better sit down."

During lunch Oliver saw Jennifer sitting with Jay and Paul.

"Look," he said to Matthew. "What do you think they're talking about?"

"Who knows?" said Matthew. "Sometimes Jennifer can be really weird."

Rusty came over to Oliver's table. "How's my stuffed owl?" he asked.

"Fine, thank you," Oliver said. "How's my bicycle?"

Rusty snorted and walked away.

After school Oliver and Sam rushed home.

"Let's hurry, Pom-pom," said Sam. She picked him up.

Oliver shoved a few Doggy Treats into Pom-pom's mouth. "Eat these, Pom-pom," he said, "for extra energy."

When they got to the parking lot, a crowd

was waiting. Josh and Kim were stringing crepe paper across the finish line. On the far side of the lot Rusty was practicing his bicycle-racing form while Jay and Paul encouraged him. Jennifer had an oversized warm-up jacket that said, "Rosemont High Pep Girl." She was stretching and doing warm-ups.

"She borrowed that jacket from her cousin in high school," said Sam.

"Yoo-hoo, Oliver," Jennifer called. "It's never too late to back out." She did a high kick. "Go—Rusty—go!" she yelled.

Oliver and Sam looked down at Pom-pom. "I sure hope this works," said Oliver.

"Me, too," said Sam. They searched the crowd.

"I don't see him," said Oliver.

"Don't worry. He'll be here," replied Sam. "And I have this." She waved a shopping bag.

Oliver heard someone call his name. "Matthew!" he said, turning around. "What are you doing here?"

"I quit," said Matthew.

"Choir practice?" asked Oliver.

"And karate and piano. It was too much. I had a long talk with my parents, and we decided that gymnastics and trumpet were enough for now."

"I'm glad you're here," said Oliver.

"We can use your help," added Sam.

Rusty rode up on his bicycle. "Let's get this over with, turkey."

"One more minute," said Oliver. "We have to

get Pom-pom ready." His eyes scanned the crowd.

"There he is," Oliver said. "Come on." Matthew, Pom-pom, Sam, and Oliver pushed their way through the crowd.

"Look at that huge dog over there," said a sixth-grader named Tiffany.

"That's Wally's dog," said her friend Jane.

"Hello, Moffitt," said Wally. Bruiser wagged his tail at Sam and Oliver.

"The race is supposed to begin in five minutes," said Sam. "Let's get started." She kneeled. "Oliver, you hold Pom-pom while Wally watches Bruiser."

Sam pulled out Pom-pom's blue satin pillow and one of Mrs. Moffitt's long scarves from her bag. "Matthew," she said, "help me tie this pillow onto Bruiser's back." Bruiser pulled on his leash and whined a little. "Good dog," Sam whispered. Wally fed Bruiser a marshmallow to quiet him.

"Now for Pom-pom," said Sam. "Oliver, just set him down on the pillow the way we practiced yesterday. Matthew and I will tie him on."

Matthew looked at the two dogs. "Pom-pom is going to race riding on Bruiser's back?"

Sam leaned over and scratched Pom-pom's head. "Don't worry," she said. "He won't fall off. He's tied on tight." Sam stood up. "I'll see you at the finish line." She disappeared into the crowd.

Wally and Oliver led the dogs to the starting line.

"Stand back! Watch out!" said Matthew. "Racers coming through!"

"That's a great idea," Oliver heard a fourth-grader say. "Rusty doesn't stand a chance now."

"I don't know," said Tiffany. "Wally's dog isn't that fast. Rusty can still beat him."

"It's going to be a close race," Jane said.

"Hi, Oliver," said Kim. "What a crazy idea. Do you think it'll work?"

"We sure hope so," answered Matthew.

"Matthew! What are you doing here?" asked Kim.

"I came to cheer," he said.

"Great," said Kim. "Come with me. I'm going over to stand near the finish line."

"Good luck, Oliver," they both shouted.

Rusty stormed over. His face was red. "What do you think you're doing?" he yelled. "That little dog isn't allowed to ride Bruiser!"

"Why not?" said Oliver. "You're riding your bike."

"But you gave me that advantage," said Rusty.

Wally stepped between Rusty and Oliver. "Do you have a problem, Jackson?" asked Wally.

Rusty looked up at Wally and scowled.

Wally continued. "I thought you told my friend Moffitt here that you could outrace *any* dog."

"I did," muttered Rusty.

"Then what are we waiting for?" Wally asked. The crowd started to laugh.

Rusty spun around angrily. "Where's the judge?" he said. Josh came forward.

"Sorry, Rusty," Josh said. "I did hear you say

you could outrace any dog when we were at the Quick Shoppe."

Rusty's face got redder. He stalked to his bicycle and climbed on. "This is the fastest bike in school," he said. "And I'm going to prove it." He hunched over the handlebars.

"Hurray for Rusty! Let's go Rusty!" shouted Jennifer, Jay, and Paul.

"Go, Pom-pom, go!" yelled Kim and Matthew.

Josh called out the instructions. "The first one to cross the finish line wins," he said. "Are you ready?"

Oliver saw Sam at the other end of the parking lot. She waved. "We're ready," he said. Rusty gripped his handlebars and nodded.

Josh began to count. "Get on your mark . . . get set . . ."

At the finish line Sam opened the shopping bag and pulled out a gallon of fudge ripple ice cream. Bruiser looked up and sniffed.

"Go!" yelled Josh.

Bruiser let out a bark of joy and took off. Rusty pedaled furiously alongside him. The crowd leaned forward to watch. Bruiser galloped toward Sam.

"Oh, no," cried Oliver. "Pom-pom's saddle is slipping. Hang on, Pom-pom!" he shouted.

"Rusty just pulled ahead," said Tiffany. "Pom-pom's having trouble holding on."

"No. Wait," said Jane. "It's okay! He's tied tight. Pom-pom and Bruiser are back in the lead. They're going to make it!"

"Hurry, Pom-pom," yelled Oliver. "You're almost there!"

Bruiser and Pom-pom tore through the crepe paper.

"The winner!" yelled Josh. The crowd cheered. Bruiser buried his face in fudge ripple.

A second later Rusty crossed the finish line. He jumped off his bicycle and threw it to the ground. "No fair!" he shouted. "That was an unfair race."

No one was listening. Jay, Paul, and Jennifer ran over to him. "What happened?" asked Jay.

"I thought you had the fastest bike in school," said Jennifer. "I wasted my best cheers on you." She stalked off.

Oliver ran over and untied Pom-pom. He was nearly upside down under Bruiser. He looked a little seasick. Oliver hugged the little dog. "Thanks, Pom-pom," he said. "You were wonderful." Pom-pom wagged his tail.

Oliver's friends crowded around to congratulate him. "Good work," shouted Matthew.

"We did it," said Sam.

"Let's hear it for Pom-pom and Bruiser," Kim yelled.

Oliver turned to Wally. "Thanks, Wally," he said. "We couldn't have done it without Bruiser."

"Don't mention it, Moffitt," said Wally. Bruiser looked up from the fudge ripple and wagged his tail.

"Yoo-hoo, Oliver," Jennifer waved. "Would you give me one of your flyers? Just in case

Princess Fluffy needs someone to look after her."
She joined the group.

Oliver walked over to Rusty. He was complaining to Jay and Paul about the race.

"What do you want?" Rusty said to Oliver. "Did you come to take my bike away?"

"Not really," replied Oliver.

Rusty looked at him suspiciously. "What do you mean?" he asked.

"Look, Rusty," said Oliver. "I'm a pet-care expert. What am I going to do with another bike? Why don't we just forget the whole thing?"

Rusty shrugged. "Fine by me," he said. "The seat's too high for you anyway."

Oliver looked at Rusty and shook his head. "See you around." Then he turned to his friends. "How about a celebration? We'll go to Sundae City! Fudge ripple triple-deckers for everyone! You, too, Pom-pom."

That night at dinner, Oliver gave half his hamburger and all his peas to Pom-pom. Pom-pom just looked at the food.

"How was school today?" asked Mrs. Moffitt.

"Great," answered Oliver. "Business is picking up, too."

"That's wonderful," said Mrs. Moffitt. "Did Wally give you a good recommendation?"

"The best," replied Oliver. "May I be excused from the table now? I promised Pom-pom a ride in my bike basket before it gets dark."

"I'm so happy you and Pom-pom are getting along so well," said Mrs. Moffitt.

"He's okay," Oliver replied. "A little dog is a lot easier to take care of." Oliver got up from the table. "Let's go, Pom-pom," he said.

"Don't be long," said Mrs. Moffitt. "I have ice cream for dessert. Fudge ripple."

"Fudge ripple?" said Oliver. He rolled his eyes.

"But I thought you liked ice cream," said Mrs. Moffitt.

"I do," said Oliver. "But tonight I think I'll give my helping to Pom-pom. After all, he deserves it."

Pom-pom rolled over and whimpered. "Just kidding, Pom-pom," said Oliver with a smile. "Let's go for our ride."